Rural Decay

An Extreme Horror Novella by

Jason Nickey

Copyright © 2024 by Jason Nickey

All rights reserved.

No part of this publication may be reproduced, distributed, or transmitted in any form or by any means, including photocopying, recording, or other electronic or mechanical methods, without the prior written permission of the publisher, except as permitted by U.S. copyright law. For permission requests, contact bibliobeard@gmail.com

The story, all names, characters, and incidents portrayed in this production are fictitious. No identification with actual persons (living or deceased), places, buildings, and products is intended or should be inferred.

Book Cover by Jason Nickey

First edition 2024

Blurbs

"A cacophony of terror and unapologetic brutality, akin to a freshly opened wound dripping with thrill and unease."

-Carietta Dorsch, author of 'Unmarked Grave'

"This book packs a punch with the violence and gore but also holds a well written plot that captivates you."

-Asher Dark, author of 'Gothic Filth'

"I felt like I was grinding my teeth the whole time while reading this. It's a twisted tale of father and son like you've never read before."

-Dan Shrader, author of 'Soulless Lonesome'

RURAL DECAY

"Rural Decay doesn't come out swinging. Instead, it charges at you with a fucking chainsaw!"

-Stuart Bray, Author of 'Violence On The Meek'

For the Modern Grotesque crew. It's been an honor working with you and getting to know you. You know who you are, you sick fucks!

Foreword

A Warning

I've stated before in previous books of mine that, as a writer, I never want to be pigeonholed into any specific subgenre of horror. I enjoy writing all different types of stories that range from the mild to the extreme. If the warning on the cover didn't tell you, this story is an extreme one. In fact, it's the most extreme piece of fiction I've written since the latter half of 'When The Mockingbird Sings', which I co-authored with Stuart Bray.

I actually wrote this story about a year ago but didn't feel very confident about it. I knew there was something here, but it didn't quite feel ready yet. Then, Jonathan Butcher (appropriate surname), a legend in the genre, was nice enough to proofread it for me and give some advice and suggestions on how to improve it. It goes without saying that I both respect and admire this man and his writing, so I took what he said to heart.

What I hope I've created here is a story that will make the regular splatterpunk readers smile with twisted delight, but also give them something unlike things they've read before.

If you're not a regular splatterpunk reader, this story contains graphic violence and sexual assault, and may not be for you. But rest assured, I have plenty of stories out there that don't push the boundaries this one does.

Contents

1. The Monster's Son   1
2. Batter Up   19
3. Pretty Woman   27
4. Arrested Development   39
5. Derailed   49
6. A New Home   57
7. Rude Awakening   69
8. Decay   79
Acknowledgements   83
Also by   85
About the author   87

1

The Monster's Son

"Hey, you're that murderer's son, aren't you?"

A phrase I sometimes wonder if I would have grown used to hearing. If things hadn't ended the way they did, I'm sure I would have heard it often. What may surprise people is that it wouldn't have bothered me. In fact, it never did. You see, my father was a serial killer, and he was also my hero.

I've always looked up to my father, even after I found out he was a serial killer. When I discovered this, rather than being scared off, it only made me look up to him more. His passion and dedication to what he did was admirable. As far back as I can remember, he was, to me, the epitome of what a man should be. With his deep voice, football player frame, bushy beard, and thick pelt of chest hair... he just emanated masculinity.

One of my earliest memories of him was falling down the front steps as a toddler. I lay there, crying, and he looked down at me with concern, "Jack, are you okay?" He quickly came down the stairs, scooped me up in his massive arms, and held me. "It's okay, little buddy. You're okay."

I felt so safe in those arms; like nothing could ever hurt me. I believe it was at that moment that my main desire in life was to be just like him. Even walking in on him slaughtering a woman didn't change that.

To say my childhood was different from most would be one hell of an understatement. My mother died when I was very young, so it was just my dad and I for most of my life. Most of the time, we lived what seemed like a normal everyday life. He would drop me off at school on his way to work and pick me up at the library that sat next to my school when he got off. We did everything together, and he was always good to me.

The only variance we seemed to have over most kids with a single father was that there were occasions where he would lock me in my room for the majority of the day. He would always leave me with stuff to drink and snack on in case I needed it, and before he would leave, he would kiss me on the forehead and tell me it was all for my own safety.

As soon as he would leave, I'd run to my window and watch him wander off into the woods behind our house. I knew he was heading off to the cabin that sat a few hundred yards behind our house, but I never knew what he did there. I would rack my brain trying to think of the different things he could be doing back there, wondering why I would need to be locked in my room to be safe.

I learned quickly not to ask him about it, because he would never disclose anything. If I tried to push the issue, he would get very stern with me, and I hated nothing more than my dad being upset with me.

"I told you, Jack. Daddy has business to attend to. It's adult stuff, but we can watch a movie together tomorrow. Okay?"

I'd nod when he would say that, but I still hated any moment I had to spend away from him.

During these times when he would leave me in my room, I did my best to just play with my toys and have fun. However, I never stopped wondering what it could be that he was doing out there in the woods behind our house. By the time I was seven, my curiosity got the best of me, and I devised a plan to find out.

I had recently seen a cartoon where a person tied their sheets together like a rope and used it to climb out of a window, so I decided I would try this myself. Shortly after he left, I ran to my window to watch him walk off into the woods. Once I could no longer see him, I pulled my sheets off the bed and tied them together. I then tied one end to the leg of my bed and threw the other out of the window. The window sat about twelve feet off the ground, so the sheets were just long enough to get me most of the way down.

With shaky arms and legs, I slowly worked my way down my makeshift rope. I made it most of the way before discovering that my knot tying abilities weren't the best. The knot that held the sheets together gave way, and I fell about five feet to the ground, landing on my butt. I worried about how I would get back in now without him noticing. I worried about him seeing my sheet hanging out of the window and finding me outside, knowing that I had disobeyed him. I was so afraid he would be mad at me, I almost started crying.

My curiosity outweighed my fear though, and it wasn't long before I braved the walk through the woods to what would be later labeled 'The Murder Cabin' in news reports.

Being only seven years old at the time, making my way through the woods by myself was kind of scary. I kept jumping at every noise and looking over my shoulder, wondering if something was about to jump out at me.

As I approached the cabin, I began to hear strange noises. I knew the one noise to be my dad grunting, but the other sounded like a woman trying to scream. My heart began racing, my hands shaking as I crept up to the cabin. The door was sitting partway open, so I peeked my head in. The inside of the cabin was very rustic and looked to be rarely used. Cobwebs infested nearly every corner, and layers of dust sat on most of the floor.

I looked off into the corner of the room and saw a woman tied to what looked like a bigger version of a sawhorse. Her arms and legs were tied to the legs of the sawhorse, and she had a cloth in her mouth that was tied at the back of her head. Her face was bright red, and she was sweating. The look on her face was one of fear. She looked as though she had been straining, and in an immense amount of pain.

My dad stood beside her, slowly stripping off his clothes. I had seen him naked around the house before, but this was the first time I had seen him with his penis erect. Seeing that, along with the naked woman gave me even more of a sense of excitement, that thrill of seeing something you weren't supposed to be seeing. It was similar to the way I felt when I watched one of his porno tapes a few weeks earlier. I knew it was something I wasn't supposed to be watching, and that I would get in trouble if he found out, but that only made the whole thing more thrilling.

I watched as he made his way around to her ass and shoved himself inside her. From the video I had seen before, I knew what he was doing. But unlike the women in said video, this woman clearly wasn't enjoying what he was doing.

With his focus on the woman, he didn't notice me slowly approaching. The woman did though, and her eyes went wide at the sight of me. Struggling against the cloth that was gagging her, she managed to push it out of her mouth with her tongue.

"Kid! Help me! Go call for help! Please!" She screamed.

My dad jumped back at the sight of me, startled. The look of both fear and disappointment on his face was overwhelming to me, and I wanted to do something to let him know that I wanted to help, just like I did with most things around the house. Whether it was cleaning the house, working on his truck, or running errands, we did everything together. It only seemed right that we do this together too.

Thinking quickly, I ran to the woman and grabbed the cloth that she had pushed out. "What are you doing? You need to get help! Ple-"

Before she could finish her sentence, I worked the cloth back into her mouth and stepped back to watch my dad finish what he was doing. He gave me a surprised nod of approval and went back to fucking her.

I sat, cross legged on the floor, my chin resting in my hands, and watched my dad inflict pain on this strange woman. As a smile formed on my face, the look of fright on the woman's face intensified.

After a few minutes, the look on my dad's face changed. He began grunting in a different way and closed his eyes. With a few loud grunts, he stopped for a moment to catch his breath before pulling out and stepping back from her. He waved me over and led me to a counter at the far wall of the cabin.

An array of large metal tools lay strewn about. A wrench, a sledgehammer, an ax, a hack saw, and hedge trimmers. I had seen him use these for different tasks around the house before, but I wasn't sure why he was bringing me over to them. I looked over the tools, then back to my dad. With a smile, he said, "Pick one."

I looked over them once more, before settling on the hedge trimmers.

"Good choice, Jack. You can really have fun with these."

"Really?" I asked with a smile.

"Uh-huh. Watch this."

With the hedge trimmers in hand, he walked back to the woman. I followed just behind him. He knelt down by her arm, which was tied to the leg of the sawhorse at the wrist. Opening the trimmers, he slid the bottom blade below her fingers, just under the bottom joint.

"You know how we use these to trim the hedges every summer?" he asked.

"Yeah."

"Well, think of this lady's fingers as those hedges. They're in the way, and we don't need them."

"But won't that hurt her?"

"That doesn't matter, buddy. She was only here to make daddy feel good. We have no use for her anymore."

My confusion must have been obvious, because he continued, "Some men like to keep women around all the time. But some men, the ones like me, only need them for one thing. Once they're done, it's time to get rid of them."

I didn't understand what he meant, but I also didn't want him to be disappointed, so I nodded my head.

"You ready?"

I nodded again.

I saw his big hands grip the handles tight and pull the trimmers together, cutting off the woman's fingers as if they were made of paper. She let out a scream unlike anything I had heard before. Blood sprayed from her hand as her fingers rolled around on the floor.

Fascinated, I walked over to the fingers and picked them up off the floor. I had seen him cut up deer for meat after hunting, but it was a whole new experience seeing what a person's tissue and bone looked like in real life.

"Can I keep these?" I asked.

He looked at me with a sense of pride that I could feel down in my soul before shaking his head with a chuckle. "Sorry, Bud. We can't keep any pieces of her, but I have a better idea."

I followed him as he stepped back behind the woman and got down to his knees again, bringing himself to my level. "Put them in here" he said, pointing between the woman's legs. The pink hole he was pointing to was leaking, and it reminded me of a drooling mouth. I gave him a curious look.

"Go ahead. It's okay," he said with a nod.

I began inserting the woman's fingers, one by one into the hole between her legs. As soon as I was done, he pulled me in for a hug and kissed me on the forehead. "I'm so proud of you, son," he said, before pulling away and giving me a serious look. "But we can never tell anyone about what goes on in this cabin. If you tell anyone, they'll take Daddy away from you. Okay?"

I nodded, fear filling my heart and tears beginning to form in my eyes.

"Don't cry, buddy. Daddy knows what he's doing. As long as you keep it our secret, we'll be fine."

The woman must have worked the cloth out of her mouth again, because she began spouting off. "You sick fuck! How can you teach your son this shit? You need to be locked away and he's gonna need a fucking therapist!"

I cringed at her yelling. This whole experience was overwhelming. It was like a sensory overload. The only thing keeping me from being scared was knowing I was safe with my dad, so I didn't like hearing her talk about him this way.

He grabbed my chin and turned my head to face him. "You wanna help me shut her up?"

I nodded, and he stepped behind me, placing the trimmers in my hands. Still on his knees, he pulled me in, so my back was against his chest and grabbed both of my wrists, holding them tightly on the trimmers.

"I'm gonna count to three, and we're gonna put these in there," he said, pointing to her asshole.

I nodded.

"One... Two... Three"

Together, we thrusted forward, him providing most of the force as the trimmers went into her asshole all the way to the handles.

She let out another scream, this one even more shrill than the last, and her body began twitching. Blood began pouring from her as we pulled the trimmers back out.

"I'll take it from here," he said, as he took the trimmers from my hands.

Walking back toward her head, he held the trimmers in one hand and grabbed her hair with the other. He pulled her head up by the hair, and forcefully jammed the trimmers up under her chin. Blood poured from her mouth and nose as her body began twitching even more rapidly.

Still holding her by the hair, he pulled down on the trimmers, removing them from the underside of her jaw. A torrent of blood followed as the trimmers exited, making a huge puddle on the floor. Her twitching only lasted a few more seconds before she finally died.

Dad sat me in the corner of the cabin while he began cleaning up. He grabbed a large saw and began cutting her body into smaller pieces. I was able to help out some, putting those pieces into the wheelbarrow he had brought in. I even followed him out into the woods to bury her body parts in different places. I was fascinated watching him do all of this, and it felt like a new bonding experience for both of us. I only hoped that going forward, he would let me join him when he did this rather than locking me in my room. I wanted to spend every waking moment I could with my dad.

Once everything was cleaned up and we were finished, we headed back to the house to have dinner. We had a long talk after dinner, in which he explained everything to me in the best way he could, considering how young I was.

"You see, son. Daddy has urges... urges that most people in life don't have. It's kind of like when you feel hungry and want to eat, only it isn't food that I want. I don't act on these urges a lot, and I try to be smart about it when I do, because I don't want to get caught. I don't want to be taken away from you. That's why

I bring these ladies here, so I can have my fun and get rid of them before anyone even notices they're gone."

After a moment of silence, I asked, "What were you doing when I first got there? It looked like you were just bumping into her from behind."

I didn't mention that I had seen it in one of his movies before, but I was also curious why two people would do that.

He paused for a while, thinking about how to answer that question. "That's... that's something grown-ups do. It's something you won't be ready for until you're older, but when you are, I'll teach you what to do."

While I couldn't grasp the magnitude of it, I understood him better than one would assume a child could. I think the fact that I not only enjoyed watching what he did, but also wanted to contribute speaks to the fact that whatever was inside him that made him have these urges was also inside me to some extent. I had strange urges myself too, like wanting to play with the insides when he would field dress a deer.

As time went on, and I grew to understand things more, I realized that he was very smart about how he did everything. We lived at the end of a desolate holler in rural West Virginia. That, along with his 'murder cabin' being in the woods behind our house, meant there was no chance that anyone would ever see or hear what he was doing out there. When he would pick a day to act out his urges, he would take the day off work and go into the city, usually picking one of the slummier areas. The women he would grab were usually street walkers or addicts, typically trashy in appearance. At the time, I always just thought they looked sick or tired. I figured that's why their arms were sometimes scabbed up or why they were so skinny. I didn't realize they were chosen this way on purpose because they were less likely to be reported as missing quickly, if at all.

Even after he explained his process to me later that night, it wasn't something I fully understood until I got a bit older.

He told me that sometimes, he could simply lure them into his car and just drive them to the house with the offer of money or drugs, but others, he would have to knock them out and tie them up, driving them home in cab of his truck.

I wondered if this was why my mother was no longer around. I asked him about this a few times, but he would usually shy away from the answer. I wouldn't learn the truth about what happened to her until much later.

2

Batter Up

After the day I discovered my dad in the cabin with that woman, life mostly went back to normal. We didn't talk about it much. I tried to ask questions here and there, but he told me that if we talked about it too often, there would be more of a chance of it slipping out when we didn't want it to.

It was a few months later when he acted on his urge again. I had gotten off school and was walking over toward the library. I heard a horn honk and looked over to see my dad already waiting for me. I immediately ran over to his truck and hopped in.

"I have a surprise for you at home."

"A new bike?" I asked.

"No, something different. Something just for you and me," he said with a wink.

My eyes lit up at this. I sat in my seat, swinging my legs back and forth with excitement. With a smile on his face, he reached over and squeezed my leg just above the knee. In my excitement, I wanted to start asking questions, but opted not to as I didn't want to spoil the mood.

When we got home, I followed him as he carried my backpack into the house. After sitting it down, he got down to my level on one knee and looked me directly in my eyes.

"Now, when we get there, I'm gonna have my adult fun first, okay?"

I nodded.

"You can watch, but you can't help while I'm doing that. Once I'm done, then you can come over and help me with the rest. You ready, buddy?"

"Yes, daddy" I said, beaming with excitement.

He held my hand as we walked through the woods back to the cabin. We stepped in to see the woman already tied to the sawhorse. This lady had longer hair than the first, and more marks all over her body. She was also wearing a lot more make-up. The way it was smeared on her face from her crying looked strange to me. She almost looked like one of the creepy clowns I had seen at the circus before.

She began screaming through her gag as soon as the door opened. I walked alongside him as he approached her until we got about ten feet from her and stopped.

"Go ahead and sit down, buddy. I'll try not to take too long."

I did as I was told and watched as he stepped over towards the woman and began taking his clothes off. She looked at me with pleading eyes, wanting me to untie her or go run for help, but I barely noticed, distracted by my father's manly form standing before me. His cock, which appeared massive to me, especially at that age, swung as he set his clothes up on the shelf and positioned himself beside her. He looked like one of the superheroes I would often see on my morning cartoons, or the tough guy characters in action movies. The men in those movies and cartoons were often shirtless, showing their muscular physique. They were depicted as the epitome of masculinity. I always viewed him the same way. And even though I still had a minimal understanding of what he was doing, I found myself fascinated by it.

Standing behind the woman, he spit in is hand and shoved himself forward. The woman's eyes went wide as he entered her, a combination of shock and pain. I hardly noticed her screams and expressions of anguish as I was too distracted watching my father thrust himself in and out of her. The sweat glistening on his hairy body as he turned from man to animal with deviant lust. He growled like a bear as he came inside her, pulling back and panting afterward. I got up to walk over to him, but he held a finger up, signaling me to give him a minute. I sat back down, and he stood there, catching his breath.

He eventually cooled off and waved me over to join him. Like before, he motioned to the row of tools and asked me to pick one. I eyed the hedge trimmers again, but he stopped me before I could speak.

"We used those last time, buddy. Let's try something different."

"What about this one?" I asked, pointing to the large, rusty wrench.

"Excellent choice," he said, picking it up and handing it to me.

I dropped it immediately, my small hands and lack of strength unable to hold its weight. He laughed, "Yeah, I didn't think you would be able to grip that." He looked around for a moment before saying, "Hold on."

He ran over to a small closet that sat at the other end of the cabin and returned with an aluminum baseball bat. "Remember a while back when I taught you how to hit a ball?"

I nodded.

"Pretend she's the ball."

I grabbed the bat and walked over to the woman. I looked her body up and down before looking back at him. Already knowing the question that was forming in my head, he answered, "Wherever you want, buddy. It's our game now."

Standing at her midsection, I lifted the bat over my head and brought it down on her back. She screamed in pain, tears dripping from her face, "Why are you doing this? Please! Go get help!"

Her scream brought me more excitement, and I made my way over to her head. I brought the bat back, ready to swing. I looked at my dad. He nodded with a smile of approval. He took a pitcher stance and drew his hand back, as if ready to throw an imaginary ball.

"Here comes the pitch," he said, before bringing his arm forward in a throwing motion.

Looking the woman directly in her eyes, I could see the pleading behind them, and flashed a smile at her as I swung the bat with all my might. The aluminum made a ping sound as it cracked against her skull. Looking back, I know my swing wasn't enough to cause much, if any damage, but it at least made her see stars.

She began hyperventilating, anticipating what was to come next. Before I could swing again, I noticed that my dad now had the wrench in his hand. He held the wrench up high and brought it down on her spine.

I heard the crunch of bones and cartilage as it made contact. Her bowels released at this. Dad stepped back quickly to avoid being hit by any of it. I noticed a stream of piss running down her leg too.

"Ewww!" I said, pointing at the shit that now lay on the floor.

Dad laughed at this. "Yeah, they usually shit themselves once you start having some fun with them. Just gotta make sure you get out of the way," he said, before looking down at her. "You done?"

She didn't move or respond. She was still breathing, but she just lay there, limp and sobbing.

"Bitch, I'm talking to you! You better answer me. Don't you dare disrespect me in front of my son. Are ... you ... done!?"

She nodded, trembling.

"Say goodnight, bitch!" he said, lifting the wrench over his head.

"Goodnight, bitch," I said, not realizing he was saying it to her and not me.

He almost dropped the wrench, laughing. "I was talking to her, buddy." He said, before lifting the wrench once again. He brought it down with force on the back of her head. He lifted the wrench and struck her a few more times in different places on her head.

The crunching sound her skull made along with how misshapen her head was when he had finished made me gasp with excitement. Her head was all smashed up, and she was still breathing. I had the urge to touch her disfigured head, to play around with the pieces that had come off.

Waving me over once more, I approached my dad. He handed me a small knife and pointed to a spot on her neck. "Just shove it in here and that should finish her off. She's a fighter. You get those once in a while."

I held the knife with both hands against where he had pointed and pushed my weight into it. It was a surreal experience feeling the knife penetrate her, and I couldn't stop thinking about it for a long time.

Our clean-up went a little faster than the first time, and it continued to get quicker as we killed more women together.

3

Pretty Woman

About a year and a few women later, my dad pulled me aside to plan his next venture.

"I want to try something different this time, and I need you to help me."

"What do you want me to do?" I asked.

"Well, son, I know you're young, but I'm sure you've noticed that the women I've been bringing home aren't exactly pretty ones. They just happen to be the ones that are easier to catch. I want to... upgrade for this next one, and I think I can use you as bait."

Down at my level, he went on to explain his plan to me. I agreed to it, and a few days later, he let me stay home from school so we could put his plan into action.

He drove us down a road that sat beside a dense patch of trees. Parking the truck in a gravel lot, we made our way into the woods. About halfway, we came across a muddy spot. Already wearing old, worn-out clothes, he had me roll around in the mud and dirt some, giving me the appearance of a kid that had gotten lost and been away for a while. We then made our way to the other end of the patch of woods which opened up to a playground.

We waited, hiding behind trees until we saw a woman enter the playground with her daughter. The woman sat on a bench reading a book, barely paying any mind to her daughter, who looked to be about my age. Giving me the signal, Dad nudged me from behind the tree and I stepped out of the woods to approach the woman. Being a good little actor, I turned on the tears as I approached her and started breathing in a sporadic pattern as if I had been crying for a while. I have to admit, even at that age, I could tell she was much prettier than the other women he had brought home. She had that suburban housewife look. Her face wasn't rough or rugged from a tough life or drug use, her makeup wasn't overdone like a whore, and her hair wasn't done in a half-assed way.

Dropping her book, the woman looked at me, almost in shock as I approached. "Are you okay? What's wrong?"

"My- my friend hurt himself," I said, pointing to the trees. "Back in the woods over there. I think he needs he- help."

"Oh my god! Let me see him!" She said, standing up. Before following me into the woods, she turned to her daughter, "Honey, you stay right there. Mommy will be right back."

Following me into the woods, she started asking questions. "How far back is he? What happened to him?"

I just kept leading her deeper into the woods, making sure to keep making crying noises.

Once we got to out of sight from the playground, Dad popped out from behind a tree.

"Where have you been? I've been worried sick!"

"Is this your son?" the woman asked.

"Yes. His mother and I have been calling for him for an hour," he said, before looking down at me. "You know you're not supposed to leave the yard."

He grabbed me by the shirt collar and started dragging me through the woods.

"Wait! Sir! Stop!"

Dad turned to face her.

"He said his friend is hurt. He was taking me to him to help."

"Did he now?" Dad asked.

The woman stood with a confused look on her face as Dad gave her a sinister grin. The look on her face quickly changed to dread as she looked around and realized there was nobody else around.

"I... uhh... think I'm gonna head back to my daughter and make sure she's okay."

She turned to walk away, and Dad ran up to her, grabbing her from behind. As soon as he had her in his grip, he pulled a cloth from his pocket and held it over her mouth and nose.

"The fuck you are," he said. She struggled against his grip for a few minutes, but he was much larger than her. Eventually, her body fell limp.

I helped him gag her and tie her hands and feet up while she was unconscious. Once we were done, he picked her up and carried her over his shoulder. I followed him as he began walking back to the truck. Off in the distance, I could hear her daughter calling out to her, though faintly.

As we approached the road, Dad stayed within the tree line and had me open the door to the truck. After looking around to make sure the coast was clear, I waved him over. With the woman still over his shoulder, he ran to the truck and tossed her in the cab, covering her up with a dark blanket. I hopped in the door and moved over to the passenger side while he started the truck and took off to head back home.

"I've got a few more surprises for you. Some new things to try," he said, smiling at me as he drove us home. I smiled, feeling a bit excited, though it was less about what we would do to this woman once we got her home. It was more about the excitement on dad's face.

The woman started coming to just as we turned onto the road that led to our holler. She gasped and moaned at every bump we hit on the rough dirt road that led to our house. I giggled at the sounds she was making, which put a smile on my dad's face.

The woman began kicking and screaming as soon as my dad pulled her out of the truck. He appeared to be struggling to walk as we made our way into the woods, her kicking and flailing knocking him off balance.

"Bitch, if you don't calm the fuck down right now, I will drag you with a rope. You hear me?" She froze at this, whimpering the rest of the way to the cabin.

Once we had her in the cabin and tied up to the sawhorse, dad walked over the closet he had pulled the baseball bat from that previous time. He pulled out a camcorder and a tripod and set it up in front of the woman.

"I got this for us. That way, we can watch it together later."

I lit up at this. I loved the thought of sitting on the couch together and watching it at some point. It would really help on the times between each woman. Especially as we eventually had more tapes.

In the time since we first started doing this together, rather than just sitting in one spot, I slowly started getting up while he was having his 'adult fun' with the women. Seeing it from different angles, building my curiosity of what it was exactly that he got out of doing it. I thought it would bother him, but he didn't seem to mind. This time, however, I actually crawled underneath and tried to watch from below. This seemed to bother him, as he paused for a moment to nudge me away with his foot. I didn't understand why that particular position bothered him, but I didn't want to upset him, so I moved quickly and went back to where I usually sat.

Once he was finished with this part of our routine, he went back to the closet to get the second surprise of the day.

"This isn't something you can use, at least not for a while, but I think you're gonna like this."

He came back from the closet holding a chainsaw. Both the woman and I saw it at the same time. While my eyes lit up with excitement, hers lit up with intense fear. I could hear her piss hitting the floor, having trickled down her leg.

Dad pulled on the cord, and the chainsaw roared to life. The sound was almost deafening in the cabin, but it at least drowned out her screams. Dad motioned towards her body with the chainsaw, instructing me to pick a spot. I pointed to her headfirst, but dad shook his head 'no' and mouthed "not yet". I stood there and thought for a moment before pointing to her leg.

Dad approached her and revved up the chainsaw, positioning it at the top of her leg, just below the hip. Smoke bellowed from the engine as he revved it once more and began slicing through her leg. At first, it went through smoothly, but once he hit the bone, I could see that there was resistance. His face strained a bit more, and the chainsaw made a grinding noise.

The detached limb fell forward to the floor, the ankle still tied to the leg of the sawhorse. Blood sprayed from her stump as dad made his way to the other leg, repeating the action. Once that leg was severed, he killed the chainsaw and set it down.

"Watch this," he said as he approached her arms. He untied her wrists from the sawhorse legs and lifted her torso, sitting her down on the ground.

"Crawl," he commanded.

She just lay there, face on the floor, not answering him.

He looked over at me. "She wants to do this the hard way. Grab the camera."

He went to grab the chainsaw while I got the camera off the tripod. As I turned to him, he pointed down at her, instructing me to keep it on her. I did as I was told and he pulled the cord, starting the chainsaw back up. Holding the chainsaw pointed down, he walked towards the woman, bringing it between her leg stumps, mere inches from her crotch.

Feeling the wind from the saw so close to her skin, she immediately propped herself up on her arms and began crawling away as fast as she could. Her leg stumps flailed around, scrambling to help, her brain not having registered that her legs were gone just yet. It was as if her mind was involuntarily telling them to move. Dad began showboating with the chainsaw for me as he slowly chased her around the cabin. I kept my camera on her as she continued scrambling to get away, giggling at my dad the whole time.

Finally, he seemed to grow tired of the game and set the chainsaw down on the floor, leaving it running. He grabbed me and set the camera on the floor, aimed at the chainsaw.

"When I tell you to, pull this back," he said, pointing to the throttle.

I positioned myself behind the chainsaw and did as I was told. Dad then went to the woman and grabbed her arms, pulling them in the air. He began dragging her, face-first towards the chainsaw. Once he was a few feet away, he paused and turned to look at me, giving me a nod. I pulled on the throttle, and he continued dragging her until her face met the saw. I was splattered with blood as the chainsaw obliterated her face a mere three feet away from me.

Later that night, after we got everything cleaned up, we turned on the TV to see that woman's face plastered all over the news. Her name was Mary Collingswood. There was a man on screen, crying. He had a young boy and girl with him. They were also crying. That woman was their mom.

It was in that moment, that I began to realize why this was the first, and quite possibly the last time we picked a woman up this way. Knowing this woman's name just made the whole thing more real somehow. It helped me understand why we had to keep what we did a secret. Dad emphasized that by saying, "This is what I was talking about, Jack. The other ladies, I rarely saw anything about them on the news. They were street women who lived rough lives. If they do have anyone that cares about them, the media doesn't give a shit. They're all about reporting a missing suburban housewife with money though. This is why we've got to be careful. Tonight was just a special occasion."

I nodded and he pulled me into him. I fell asleep snuggled in his arms, feeling safe and secure with my hero. If I had known what was to come, I would have made sure to appreciate the moment more.

4

Arrested Development

As the years passed on and I continued to grow, we got better and faster at the whole process, but rarely more creative. I became frustrated as my pubescent years hit and I didn't develop the way I had hoped. Hitting my teen years, I learned quickly that while my father passed down his urges to me, he didn't pass down his physical traits. The little bit of height that I gained in my teen years seemed to just stretch out the already small frame I had as a child. I wanted so badly to be a large, masculine man like my father, but I was beginning to see that it just wasn't in the cards for me. It's something I still struggle with to this day.

Something else that seemed to change during this time was that I began to find myself getting aroused when my father would have his 'adult fun' with these women. He still hadn't let me participate in it, but the truth is, I didn't want to, not in the way he would have eventually let me. I found that I wasn't envious of him fucking the women, but more envious of them getting fucked by him. I would watch his large cock going in and out of these women, and picture myself in their place. I loved and admired my father for so long, and I wanted to know what it would feel like to have him inside me. I would picture him shooting his load inside me like he did with these women. I imagined my body absorbing it, and his masculinity coursing through my veins.

By the time my teenage years had hit, I grew more and more frustrated at this desire, along with the fear I held of my father's reaction if I ever told him about it. I got to a point where I began masturbating while he was fucking the women, discreetly at first, but a bit more open with each one. The first time he noticed, he gave me a bit of a funny look, but quickly went back to what he was doing. He never addressed it after that, but in some way, I think he knew it was him that was getting me off and not the women. He just stopped looking over at me while it was happening.

I finally broke one day shortly after my seventeenth birthday and made an attempt to satiate my own desire as best I could. The way I saw it, he satisfied his urges, so why couldn't I? It wasn't even something I had planned, it just happened.

I had skipped school that day, opting to stay home. Feeling frustrated and lonely, I hopped on the four-wheeler we had recently acquired to make our trips to the cabin easier and began driving around the roads in the area. It started off as a really good way to blow off steam, but when I saw a guy walking alongside the road, instinct kicked in. I pulled off on the side of the road a few feet away from him.

"You need a lift or something?" I asked.

"Yeah, if you don't mind. I'm heading to Laurel Creek."

I stood there eying the man up. He wasn't built like my dad, but he was hairy like him and had a beard.

Much like the women we often brought home, he had a rough, trashy appearance.

"You don't happen to have any weed on you, do you? I could use a fuckin toke right now," he asked.

I knew this was my opening.

"I do, but not on me. We can swing by my place on the way. I've got a stash in the cabin behind my house."

"Fuck yeah, brother!" he exclaimed.

"Hop on."

As he was getting on the four-wheeler, his placed his hands on my hips briefly to adjust himself. My cock instantly got hard, and I knew it was my chance to try.

We made our way up the road, eventually turning up on the dirt road that led to my house. I zoomed past the house, heading into the woods toward the cabin. As we stepped inside, he had a suspicious look on his face while looking around. I let him wander around a bit while I pretended to look for the stash of weed that I didn't have before eventually cornering him over by where the sawhorse sat. I reached out and grabbed his cock through his pants. He flinched at this.

"Jesus, kid. What the fuck are you doin'?"

"You wanna fuck me?" I asked.

"What are you, like fourteen?"

"Seventeen, actually. I'm just small for my age."

"Still too fuckin' young, and besides, I ain't no faggot."

Feeling brave, I pulled my pants down and bent over the sawhorse, presenting my ass to him. "Nobody has to know. Just pretend I'm a woman."

"This is too fucked up even for me, kid. I'll just walk the rest of the way home."

"Where the fuck are you going?" I asked, anger rising inside me.

"I'm goin' home. I suggest you do the same. You're askin' to get hurt doing this crazy shit. Some of these fellas 'round here would kick your ass for this shit... or worse."

He began walking towards the door. In a rage-induced panic, I grabbed for the wrench on the counter and ran up to him. Just before he got to the door, I raised it over my head with both hands and brought it down with all I had on the top of his head. He immediately collapsed to the ground and began convulsing. I got to my knees and hit him in the head again. It took three more blows before he finally stopped moving.

I sat on the floor and cried before dragging him back in. I had no idea what to do. I didn't know how to fix this situation. There was no way I could get his body buried and clean up the mess before dad got home.

Defeated, I made my way back to the house and awaited dad's return, dreading his disappointment. I began to shudder as I heard his truck pull up. I was already breaking down by the time he got in the door.

"Shit, Jack. What's wrong?"

"I fucked up, dad. I'm sorry. I need your help."

Concerned, he asked, "What did you do?"

"I tried to do what we do, but on my own. I don't know why, I just did it. I'm sorry. I'm so so sorry."

I could tell he was upset, but he still hugged me and let me cry into his chest. Once I finally got myself to calm down, he looked me in the eyes, "Let's go out to the cabin and clean up your mess."

I nodded, and we set off into the woods.

We didn't say much as we set to work getting it cleaned up. He didn't ask why or how it happened, but I think some part of him knew. I could tell by the looks he was giving me throughout the night.

Once we had finished cleaning up, we went back into the cabin.

"We need to talk," he said in a very solemn tone. He put his hand on my shoulder and led me over to the sawhorse. He began to slowly undress me as he continued. My dick went instantly hard as he did this. I wondered if I was finally going to get what I'd been wanting for a while.

"I know that you acted on impulse, and I can understand that better than anyone, but you need to promise me this won't happen again."

I nodded.

"I'm proud of you for at least picking a drifter, but as a result of this, I'm gonna have to wait longer before I can have my own fun again."

"I'm so-"

"I don't need you to apologize, I just need you to listen."

I nodded again.

"I... I know why you picked him, why you brought him here. I know what you've been wanting. I've known for some time now. I'm going to do this for you this one time, to hopefully get it out of your system, but know that I mean it when I say this is the only time. You acted on your urge, and since I can't bring a woman here for a while to act on mine, it's going to have to be you."

He took a deep breath before continuing. I felt his hands on my head, and it took a moment for me to realize he was putting a wig on me.

"I'm going to warn you, this isn't going to feel good, though I suspect... I fear that some part of you will enjoy this. I can promise you that you won't end up like those women out in the woods. You're still my son, and I still love you. Okay?"

"I trust you."

With that, he slammed my upper body down on the sawhorse and ran a knife along my back, slicing me enough that there would be blood, but not bad enough that I would need medical attention afterwards. I then heard him spit into his hand and was overcome with an intense combination of pleasure and pain as he thrust himself inside me. Despite the pain, despite holding back screams, I felt joy. His cock felt like it was splitting me in half, but I still got an erection at the sound of his grunts and the feeling of his sweat dripping on me as he had his way with me. As he got close and grabbed my hips with his meaty hands, I came in unison with him.

He didn't say a word after he finished. He left me here on the sawhorse as he grabbed his clothes and headed back to the house. I gave him time to get back before making my way home, wanting to give him space. I had finally gotten what I wanted, and I walked home with a smile. In my mind, I kept replaying the moment he shot his seed inside me. I fantasized about his masculinity coursing through my body, wishing it would make me more like him physically.

I lay in bed that night in pain, realizing that rather than satiating my desire, what happened that night only made me want more.

The next morning, I tried to apologize again, but he cut me off.

"Let's just start over and pretend it never happened. The way you feel is probably my fault, and I'm sorry for that, but we have to go back to the way things were. What you want just... it just isn't right. Neither is what I did last night, but we can move past this, okay."

"How?" I asked.

"Maybe," he began, pausing before continuing, "Maybe we can switch it up on occasion. Bring someone back for you once in a while. You've been helping me out all this time. Maybe I need to be the one to help you sometimes."

5

Derailed

Over the course of the next few months, the awkwardness between my father and I faded, and things slowly went back to some form of normalcy. I wish I could say that it stayed this way, but once again, I seemed hellbent on destroying everything we had.

Having made plans to pick up another woman the next day, we were getting everything prepared and ready. It was the first time we had been in the cabin since the night my father took me the way he did those women. It made the emotions and desires I had been doing my best to curb come rushing back in. I spent the majority of the night trying to be mindful of the looks I gave him, just as he did his best to ignore them when they happened.

As I lay in bed that night, as I had a few times over the last year or so, I stepped out into the hallway and walked to his door. I stood in his doorway, watching him sleep, wishing I could lie next to him and be comforted by those big arms as I had when I was a child.

In his sleep, unaware of my presence, he rolled over, exposing his huge erection. Unable to control myself, I approached him slowly and climbed onto the bed next to him, watching to make sure he didn't stir. I leaned over and took him in my mouth, the way I had seen women do in movies. He began moaning softly, his hips writhing just slightly. I hoped that he was awake and enjoying himself, but that hope was busted when he realized what was happening.

He grabbed me with his meaty hands and threw me off the bed. I landed on the floor and broke down crying. He sat there, dejected, before finally speaking.

"I told you this could never happen. I love you, son, but you need to get past this. It can't happen. It won't happen."

"But what if I can't?" I asked through tears.

"Then... as much as I hate to say this, maybe we'll have to look into you living somewhere else. I'll never attempt to pretend that what we do to these women is normal, but apparently doing this together has twisted your mind in some way. This dependence you have on me isn't healthy, and I know I caused it."

"I don't want to do that."

"I don't either, Jack. You're my son and I love you, but this is going to tear us apart one way or another. I don't feel the same way as you, and I never will. Maybe you should try to get out there and meet some guys or something, see if it will help."

"I could try that again, I guess."

"Yeah, just don't kill them this time. At least not until we get this shit figured out and can plan for it," he said with a laugh, leaning forward to playfully punch me in the shoulder.

"I'm sorry again, dad."

"It's okay. Go to bed, buddy. We have a big day tomorrow."

"Can I... ask you one more thing?"

He nodded.

"What really happened to mom? You never did tell me how she died. Did... did you do it?" I looked down as I asked that last part, afraid to look him in the eyes while making that accusation.

He sighed, "No. I didn't do that. Your mother was different than the others. I wouldn't have hurt her."

"So, what happened?"

"She would often go on weekend trips to visit her mother, your grandmother, out in Kentucky. Her mother wasn't a fan of me, so I never went along with her on these trips. Once you were born, she would take you along with her. I would use these trips as my chance to take care of things without her knowing.

"On one particular trip, she had gotten into an argument with your grandmother and came home early. She became worried when she couldn't find me anywhere, despite my truck being outside, and started searching around for me. At some point, she heard a scream in the woods and went out to see what was going on. That's when she found me in the cabin with a woman, much like you did a few years later.

"She... she didn't handle it very well. Most people wouldn't. She told me she felt as if the world had crumbled around her. That night, she took a bunch of sleeping pills and slit her wrists in the bathtub."

I sat there, stunned to finally hear the truth. I had always of assumed that he probably assisted in her death in some way. I still wasn't necessarily convinced he wasn't at least somewhat involved, but I was relieved he at least told me what led to her death.

I didn't push the issue any further, but I think he knew that I still suspected he was involved somehow. I stood up and hugged him before heading back to my bedroom. It took a while but sleep eventually found me.

The next day, I stayed at the house while he went into town to pick out a woman to bring home. Later on, when he eventually came home, we headed to the cabin together and began our routine.

From the beginning, everything felt off. Unlike previous times, I resisted my urge to jerk-off while he was having his fun with the woman, opting to just operate the camera. I began to notice that he seemed to be getting frustrated, and it wasn't long before I realized that he was having trouble maintaining an erection. I knew deep down that it was because of me, because of what I had done the night before.

As his frustration grew, he looked at me with rage in his eyes. "Just turn the goddamn camera off."

I did as I was told and walked over to the closet to put it away. Hoping that it would help, I stayed on that side of the room rather than watching.

"Fuck!" he called out.

I turned to see him grab the sledgehammer, a weapon we rarely used, from the counter. In a fit of rage, he just began slamming it into her repeatedly, pummeling her over and over again until her body just looked like a meat bag.

When he was done, he threw the hammer to the floor and collapsed. For the first time in my life, I witnessed my father crying. I walked over to his side of the room and began up.

"Don't. Just don't," he said, as he stood up and headed toward the door. "Let's just go home. We'll get it tomorrow."

"Okay, dad. I'm sorry."

"I just feel distracted. I've felt that way all day. I should have waited longer."

I sheepishly followed him through the woods back to the house. My heart dropped as we approached the house and I saw flashing red and blue lights. Before I could even register what was happening, the cops tackled both of us to the ground and handcuffed us. Backup eventually arrived, and they began searching the woods. They quickly detained both of us and brought us into the station.

Apparently, still a bit shaken from the night before, Dad was thrown off and got sloppy. When he abducted the woman, not only was there a witness, but they also got his tags. To make it worse, the woman, despite being an addict, was the sister of a cop.

I sat in the station for what felt like forever. Detectives, cops, and feds all showed up to talk to my dad and question him. When he was finally let out and they walked him past me, his hands still cuffed, he gave me a knowing look and nodded. I knew in that moment that he had not only confessed, but that he was taking the fall for everything. I guess his last gift for me was my freedom, but some gift that was. I was heartbroken at the knowledge that I might never see my father again.

I wondered what was to come next. *Where would my life go? What would I do with these urges I seem to have inherited from my father? Would I ever be reunited with him?*

6

A New Home

While my father was awaiting trial, the state didn't seem to know what to do with me. I was immediately set up with a psychiatrist and put in a foster home. Being not quite eighteen yet, I was still about a year away from being able to be let out on my own, and they determined that a foster home with a reputable couple would be a better transition for me than just throwing me into a boy's home, especially considering the way the boys there might act towards me once they knew who I was.

To make things worse, they wouldn't even let me see or talk to my dad. They wanted me to see the psychiatrist they had set me up with a few times first, long enough to get a full evaluation before determining whether or not to let me see him.

The couple they had set me up with seemed kind enough, but that situation didn't last long. They looked to be in their fifties. Their own children had grown and left home over ten years ago, and they'd spent the time since fostering troubled teens here and there.

The woman, Brenda, had kind eyes and long, strawberry blonde hair. She had a little extra weight on her, but I could tell she was probably a knockout in her younger years. She hugged me as soon as she saw me, whispering in my ear that everything would be okay. She even told me that she would homeschool me to prevent the circus I would encounter with the unwanted celebrity status I had recently acquired because of my father.

Tim, her husband, didn't seem quite as kind as Brenda. She assured me that he was the strong silent type, but I could tell by the way he looked at me when we first met that he was wary of letting me into their house. He had a gruff appearance that reminded me a bit of my father, only slightly older with a touch of gray to his hair and beard.

Over the course of the first week, Tim slowly warmed up to me, and as he did so, I could see something in his eyes that I recognized. It was similar to the look my father gave the women he brought home before he fucked them. The more he looked at me with those eyes, the more I wanted him. I didn't realize it at the time, but I think I transferred my lust for my father onto him.

I spent the next few months doing everything I could to tempt him. I started off slow at first. I would walk around the house with no shirt on any time Brenda wasn't home, which was at least a few evenings a week. She was quite the bleeding heart, so she volunteered for many different church programs to help others.

I soon escalated my efforts by not wearing underwear beneath my shorts, making sure to sit in positions that left little to the imagination. Tim would do his best not to stare as I did so, but I could see him looking, and he never once requested that I go upstairs to change or put more clothes on.

I'd also occasionally ask him for help with something I was working on the computer and when he'd come over to see what the problem was, I'd make sure my hand brushed against his cock here and there. There were times I could feel it start to grow hard when I did this.

By the end of the first month, I began just walking around naked when Brenda wasn't home. The first time I did it, Tim seemed to be in shock at the sight of me. He stumbled on his words as he attempted to talk to me, but never once asked what I was doing or requested I get dressed. I'd sit at the other end of the room while he watched TV, putting myself in a place where he could easily see me, and pretend to be aloof to the fact that he kept peering over at me. I'd play with myself on occasion too, just enough to keep my cock semi erect the whole time.

On one particular night, a movie he was watching turned out to be a bit more erotic than he expected. Not only was it a sex scene, but it was a sex scene with two attractive, muscular men. As the long, passionate scene played out, I began masturbating. When I noticed him looking over at me, I made direct eye contact with him.

"This scene is hot. You wanna jack off together?" I asked.

His face turned red, and he cleared his throat before answering, "I... I don't think that would be appropriate."

"You can't tell me you aren't hard as a rock right now. Don't worry, I won't tell Brenda."

I could see hesitation in his eyes, but I could also see his desire.

"Come on, Tim. I wanna watch you play with your cock. I'll even help if you want."

His breathing got heavy, and I could tell he was nervous, but slowly, he began taking off his clothes. I made my way over to the couch and sat next to him. The head of his dick was glistening with pre-cum. I leaned over and took it in my mouth. Just as I expected, there was no protest from Tim. In fact, he was so turned on that he came very quickly. I then leaned back on the couch and began taking of myself. Even though he'd just came, he still watched me with lustful eyes as I got myself off.

After it was over, I went back to my bedroom to get dressed. Tim acted nervously when Brenda got home, as if he was afraid I'd tell her what happened, but that eased as the next few days passed.

Over the next week or two, Tim and I spent the nights we had alone together going a little further with each session. He began reciprocating my actions some, and we began kissing as if we were making love. This made me uncomfortable at first, but as it progressed, I started forgetting that my plan was just to seduce him. When I heard his moans of pleasure, I would close my eyes and picture my father standing behind me. In more intense moments, I would see the women's faces as my father had his way with them. I was enjoying my sexual encounters with Tim, but something was missing. The lack of violence after left me wanting something more.

It was about three weeks after the first time we fooled around that I finally talked Tim into fucking me. In the middle of a heated session, I got down on my knees and bent over the coffee table. I'm not even ashamed to admit that I begged him to fuck me. I had him so worked up that he wasn't even remotely reluctant to do it. He spit in his hand to lube up his cock, then shoved it inside me. I could tell this wasn't the first time he'd done this. I wondered how many men he had done this behind Brenda's back. I pictured her reaction if she ever found out, and it excited me.

I moaned with a combination of pain and pleasure, gripping the table tightly while he had his way with me. I knew it was Tim behind me, but I pictured my father the entire time. I pictured those women, bloody and mangled. It was a moment of pure ecstasy for me, which probably explains my over-the-top reaction when it was interrupted.

Apparently, whatever volunteering Brenda was doing that night ended early. We didn't even hear her car pull into the driveway, but we did hear her scream when she walked through the door to find Tim plowing me from behind over the coffee table.

At the sight of her, Tim immediately pulled out and ran into the other room. Brenda stood there at the door, a look of shock on her face.

"I think I'm going to be sick," she said, bringing her hand to her mouth.

"I... I can explain," Tim called out from the kitchen doorway.

"You don't have to explain shit to her, Tim. I'm giving you what she won't."

"Our sex life is none of your business!" she screamed, pointing at me.

"And what Tim and I do is none of yours. Why don't you go upstairs and let us finish. At least someone in this house is willing to bring your husband pleasure."

"That's it!" she screamed, pulling her phone from her purse. "I'm calling the social worker. You're gonna have to go somewhere else. You aren't welcome here anymore!"

"The fuck you are!" I said, standing up and rushing towards her. I slapped the phone out of her hand and threw her up against the door, my hand on her throat.

"I already had my father taken away from me. Now you want to take Tim away from me too? Fuck you!"

I let go of her throat and grabbed her by the hair. Pulling hard, I dragged her across the room and slammed her face down on the marble countertop between the living room and kitchen. Blood began pouring from her nose as I lifted her head and slammed it into the counter once more, harder this time. Her body went limp upon impact. I let go and watched her fall to the floor.

I knew I had fucked up. She wasn't dead, but I knew I had to get out of there. In a panic, I grabbed my clothes and took off out the door. Thankfully, it was nighttime, so I wasn't running bare-ass naked through the street in broad daylight. I made it a few houses down the road before noticing a car behind me. It had been parked near Tim and Brenda's house and began following me as soon as I started down the road. In a panic, I turned and headed into the woods so I could stop for a moment to put my clothes on.

Once dressed, I continued walking. As I made my way through the woods, paranoia began to sink in.

Every sound I heard had me looking over my shoulder, thinking the police had found me. I was sure Tim had called them by that point, so I knew they had to be looking for me. I could only imagine the news headlines. 'Son of serial murderer, Hank Buckley, on the run after assaulting foster parent.'

I wasn't familiar with this part of town, so the woods were much bigger than I realized. I walked for a good while before coming up on an old, dilapidated wooden fence. Moving one of the boards aside, I looked into the yard. The grass and shrubbery in the yard clearly hadn't been tended to for quite some time. The house didn't look to be in much better shape. With its boarded-up windows, tattered shingles, and siding that looked decades past its last paint job, it was clear the place was abandoned.

Deciding I would hide out there for the time being, I squeezed through an opening in the fence and made my way through the unkempt yard. Luckily, I was able to pry the particle board that had been nailed to the door off pretty easily. I crept inside.

The place had clearly been a den for junkies and addicts at some point, which is probably why it had been boarded up. Along with the thick layer of dust that coated the entire place, there was trash, used needles, and other drug paraphernalia strewn about the floor.

I made my way into the living room to find a ratty old couch sitting in the corner. The upholstery was torn badly, and covered with nasty-looking stains, but I deemed it better than sleeping in a jail cell for the night. I brushed the couch off a bit before laying down.

How long should I stay here? What am I going to do next? How long before they find me?

My mind raced as I lay there, but to my surprise, sleep eventually found me.

7

Rude Awakening

I had only been asleep for maybe an hour when I woke to footsteps in the other room. My blood immediately ran cold and my heart started racing. I looked around, expecting to see red and blue lights flashing, but there was only moonlight peeking through the boards on the window.

Probably just a vagrant, I thought to myself.

The footsteps entered the room I was in, and I did my best to lay still, hoping whoever it was would move on. I closed my eyes most of the way, peeking through the small opening in my eyelids so it would look as though I was sleeping.

A man in military fatigues and a black ski mask stood there in the doorway looking around. I froze when he turned towards me. There was a look in his eyes as he stood there that sent off alarm bells in my head.

"Get up," he said with a stern voice.

I opened my eyes all the way, staring directly at him. "Look, I don't want any trouble. I just needed a place to sleep, man."

"I said get up!"

I sat up and raised my hands in a surrender gesture.

He looked to his left, towards the doorway where I had entered the house. "I got him," he said with a nod to someone I couldn't see. "I figured he would end up somewhere around here after he ran into those woods."

I went to make a run for it, but only made it a few feet before he tackled me to the floor. The weight of his large frame crushed me and made it hard to breathe.

"Please, man," I pleaded, "Just let me go. I'll find somewhere else to sleep."

He kept his hold on me, and I heard more footsteps approaching. I turned my head to see another man dressed in the same fashion. He was a bit smaller than the man holding me down, and he also had a ski mask over his face. He was carrying a bag over his shoulder. He had a rag in one hand, and a bottle in the other. He uncapped the bottle and held the rag against the open mouth. Tilting the bottle, he poured whatever was into the bottle onto the rag before holding it down to my face. The chemical smell being held against my nose and mouth was overwhelming. I felt dizzy for a moment before everything went black.

Sometime later, I was shaken awake. I couldn't see. There was something over my face. It took me a moment to realize they had put a bag over my head. They had also tied my hands behind my back. I could hear an engine idling and could tell I was sitting in the bed of a truck. Hands gripped me by my armpits and my feet, lifting me into the air. I was dropped to the ground over the bed of the truck. Landing with a thud, I felt a pounding headache beginning to grow.

The two men were soon at my side, lifting me to my feet. Once standing, they removed the bag over my head. They had brought me back to my father's house... my house.

I looked at the house, lit up by the truck's headlights. Even though it had only been about two months since my dad was caught, it felt like I was starting at a relic from a lifetime ago. Hate messages were spraypainted onto the walls, words like 'murderer', 'rapist', and 'monster' standing out like a neon sign.

"Take us to the shed," the larger man said, shoving me forward.

Without saying a word, I began walking towards the woods. In the dark of the night, enhanced by the trees towering overhead, the cabin looked like a black shadow in the forest. I didn't need lights to see it, though. I knew this place like the back of my hand.

The steps creaked as we made our way up to the porch. I got the door open and hit the switch beside it, illuminating the cabin in a soft amber glow. I looked around, taking the place in for the first time since the night of the arrest. It quickly dawned on me that things were different.

For one, the sawhorse was gone. This didn't surprise me. I figured it had either been taken as evidence, or if not, someone had come and taken it either for their own morbid pleasure, or to sell.

Along with that and pretty much everything else we had in here now missing, there was also something new. Two sets of shackles had been bolted to the floor. I walked over to inspect them and felt something strike the back of my head. I immediately collapsed to the floor. The larger man climbed on top of me once more, holding me in place while the smaller man attached the shackles to my hands and feet.

Now shackled, I looked up to see the two men standing over me. "Who are you?" I asked.

They pulled off their ski masks. The larger of the two men appeared to be in his late forties. The smaller one looked to be close to my age, maybe a little older. The resemblance between them told me they were father and son.

The younger one spoke up first, "We don't look familiar? I'm sure you saw us on the news."

They did look kind of familiar. I was racking my brain trying to figure it out.

"Keep thinking, Jack. It'll come to you. Hopefully I didn't hit you too hard, motherfucker," the larger man said

Suddenly, it dawned on me. I had a flashback to sitting on the couch with my father, watching the news. I saw the face of the woman we had abducted from the park. The name on the screen; Mary Collingswood. I remembered seeing the two of them, along with the little girl from the park.

"Mary," I muttered.

"I knew you could get it. Mary was my mother. That was my little sister you two left in the park all alone."

"She was my wife," the larger man said. "I know the two of you worked together. My daughter described you to the T. Said you came out of the woods crying, saying your friend was hurt. Mary followed you into the woods to help and never came back."

I lay there, dumbfounded, unsure of what to say.

"You know, for years I had wondered what happened to her, why she was never found. When your father confessed to killing her, it didn't seem to add up. My mother was never the type to just follow a random man into the woods. Somehow, I just knew that it had to be you that baited her. She always had a soft spot for children. That was when I asked Chloe to tell me everything."

"I'm so-"

"Don't. It's my turn to talk. I also had a feeling that you weren't forced to do those things your father said. I had a gut feeling you willingly participated. I knew you were a monster too. I just had to wait for the right time get you here alone."

"So now what?" I asked.

"Ha! Now is the part where you suffer like she did."

The larger man walked over to the closet and pulled out a chainsaw. Not the one my dad had used, but a brand new one. As he revved it up, I knew what was coming, and it was no surprise when he approached my leg with ~~the~~ it in tow.

There was irony in the fact that he had just been calling me a monster, when I could see the same spark my father and I held in his eyes as he brought the chainsaw down to my leg, cutting through it like butter.

It felt like everything was in slow motion. It was as if I could feel each metal tooth of the chainsaw grinding against my flesh, muscle, and bone. Everything seemed to return to normal pace as he turned the chainsaw off and sat it on the floor. It was at that moment that I could finally hear my own screams. I was too distracted to see what the smaller man was doing as he stepped to the other side of the room.

He returned with a large frying pan that was glowing red from heat. The smell, combined with the sizzling sound as he held it against the stump of my leg almost made me pass out. I lost control of my bowels, I pissed myself, and I began vomiting from the pain.

He returned the pan back to where he had gotten it from. As he was on his way back over to me, his father was starting the chainsaw up once more. With another revving, the father raised it above my other leg and cut it off. The son repeated the same action with the frying pan immediately after.

It was at this point that they released me from the shackles and flipped me over onto my stomach. The night with my father replayed in my mind and I knew what was coming.

"Crawl!" Was all I heard the father say before the chainsaw was running once again.

They've seen the tapes, I thought to myself. *Someone found them, and they're doing to me what we did to her.*

Just like his wife had those years ago, I propped myself up onto my elbows and scrambled to get away from him as he chased me with the chainsaw.

Unlike my father, he didn't seem to get bored of it. The joy on his face never once faltered as he continued chasing me around the room, taunting me. His son was laughing and clapping the whole time. The joy he felt watching his dad get revenge was the same joy I felt watching my dad hurt those women.

It was me who eventually couldn't take the game of cat and mouse anymore. I collapsed from the combination of exhaustion and pain. When everything around me went dark, I expected that to be the end. I expected them to finish me off. I expected wrong.

8

Decay

I woke shackled to the floor once again. It took a moment to clear my mind enough to remember that I no longer had my legs. My brain eventually connected that with the pain that seemed to start at where my legs had once been and resonated through my entire body.

I lifted my head to see my legs, separate from my body, but still shackled to the floor, looking as though they had already begun to decay. I had no way of knowing how long I had been there by myself. I assumed that I had just been left there to die, either of starvation, dehydration, or infection.

The infection part was inevitable. It was almost as if I could feel it coursing through my blood like poison.

It was only a matter of time before it eventually took me.

My mind began to wander, and I could swear I saw my father enter the cabin. He didn't say a word as he approached me. He just quietly sat beside me as I looked at him with longing in my eyes, wishing I could return to the past when things were better.

Looking off into the distance, he finally spoke, "We really had something special here, Jack. I'm sorry that it's over."

He faded away before I could respond. I came to with tears in my eyes, knowing that it was just a vision, a hallucination. I was ready to accept my fate. I just wished I could see him one last time.

I faded out of consciousness again for... I don't know how long. I was pulled out of it by the two men entering the cabin. Unlike the vision of my father, I had just enough clarity to know that this was real.

Standing above me, the larger man threw a newspaper down on the floor in front of my face. I kept staring up at him.

"Look at it," he said, pointing down at the paper.

As my vision came into focus, I spotted a picture of my father on the paper. The headline beside it read, 'SERIAL KILLER HANK BUCKLEY, AWAITING TRIAL FOUND DEAD IN APPARENT SUICIDE.'

"But... but he was just here," I muttered quietly, tears forming in my eyes.

Frustrated, the father picked up the paper and held it in front of my face. "Snap out of it, Jack. Daddy's dead! And you'll be joining him soon, you sick fuck."

With that, they both left. I lay there on my back, crying, coming in and out of consciousness. I could feel myself weakening. I wondered how long I had left. I wondered how long it would be until someone found me out here. I wondered if anyone would care... Probably not. The only one who ever cared about me was now gone. I welcomed this. Everything around me was beginning to fade.

For a moment, I felt his presence near me. I felt hands grip my shoulders and turn me onto my stomach. I was ready for my father to take me like he had that one night. Then, I heard the chainsaw start up once more. I could feel the wind from the saw between my legs, coming closer.

"I'm sorry, Dad," I muttered. Then, the pain began again as the chainsaw was shoved into my ass.

Acknowledgements

As I mentioned in the forward of this book, a big thank you to Jonathan Butcher for your help and advice in improving this story.

Thank you to Stuart Bray for being a great friend, a mentor, and someone I can always bounce story ideas back and forth with.

A huge thank you to anyone who has supported me along this journey. I will always appreciate those who have taken the time to read and review my books, whether they liked them or not.

Last but not least, thank you to my Hellfire crew. You all keep me motivated and inspired to be a better person and a better writer.

Also By

Novellas:

Wreckage

Jasper And The Appalachian Zombies

Road Hazards

Collections:

Static And Other Stories

Reckless Abandon

They Come From Within

Singles:

Night Of The Living Sex Doll

Smashed. Wrecked.. Gone

Collaborations:

Hillbillies And Homicidal Maniacs (With Stuart Bray)

Hillbillies And Homicidal Maniacs Vol. 2: Horror In The Holler(With Stuart Bray)

When The Mockingbird Sings (With Stuart Bray)

Sludge (With Stuart Bray and Chuck Nasty)

Anthology Appearances:

Head Blown (Merrill David)

Head Blown Too (Merrill David)

Til Death (From The Ashes)

Harvested (From The Ashes)

Splatology (Unveiling Nightmares)

About the Author

Jason Nickey is a horror writer from Charleston, West Virginia. He is a newer writer and has mostly worked in short fiction. He is a lifelong fan of all things horror and can sometimes be found either cosplaying as Jason Voorhees or brushing his luscious beard. Links to his bigcartel store, amazon store, and other social media platforms can be found at https://linktr.ee/bibliobeard

Printed in Great Britain
by Amazon